Underground Train

Cleveland Park

Woodley Park-Zoo

Red Line

Dupont Circle

Farragut North

Metro Center

Gallery Place

Archives

Green Line

L'Enfant Plaza

Waterfront Station

My underground train path to Nana.

Underground Train

Mary Quattlebaum

illustrated by Cat Bowman Smith

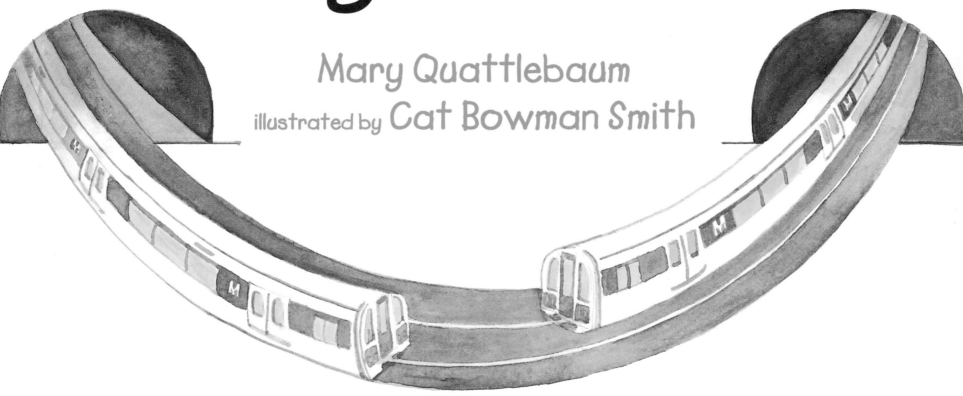

A Picture Yearling Book

Published by
Bantam Doubleday Dell Books for Young Readers
a division of
Random House, Inc.
1540 Broadway
New York, New York 10036

Visit us on the Web! www.randomhouse.com

Educators and librarians, visit the BDD Teacher's Resource Center at www.randomhouse.com/teachers

ISBN: 0-440-41325-7
Reprinted by arrangement with Doubleday Books for Young Readers
Printed in the United States of America
April 1999
10 9 8 7 6 5 4 3 2

In memory of Nana
and the thrill of trips to see her
—M.Q.

For little Gabriel,
who already knows
about underground trains
—C.B.S.

The moving stairs roll us down, down, down to the underground train, which rushes past like fast water on miles of track.

Rrrruuuummm. Whooooosshh.

I grip my fare and Mama grips my hand as the train doors slip aside like silver drapes. We step inside; the doors slide shut.

Rrrruuuummm. Whoooosshh.

The train starts slow and picks up speed.
I choose an orange seat
and watch the tunnel blurring by
like a long, black night.

Rrrruuuummm. Whoooosshh.

The train inside is filled with light.
Folks clutch their bags and smile
or read the news or yawn or talk.
The driver calls the stop:

Waterfront. Some people leave
and others take their seats;
then the bell sounds once, and the bright train starts
its rush into the dark.

Above the train, above my head, the busy city spreads: a map of tangled streets and shops, cars, buildings, flags, clocks.

Above the train, above my head, a green light turns to red.

The traffic halts; the people cross.

Some sparrows hop in lots
beside the zoo, where lions snooze

and monkeys snack on fruit,
where zebras shake their manes and neigh
high, high above the train,

which rolls below the skipping feet
of two girls leaping neat and fleet

through double ropes that smack

the sidewalk: whackity-whack!

Some kids race by on Rollerblades
and napping babies wake
with coos or cries as parents stroll

the place where Nana holds
a bag of bread and waits for me
to help her feed the geese and ducks.

Oh, high, high, high above,
the busy city moves
and shoves, skips, snacks, waits—

while down below, the train goes fast, fast, fast through miles

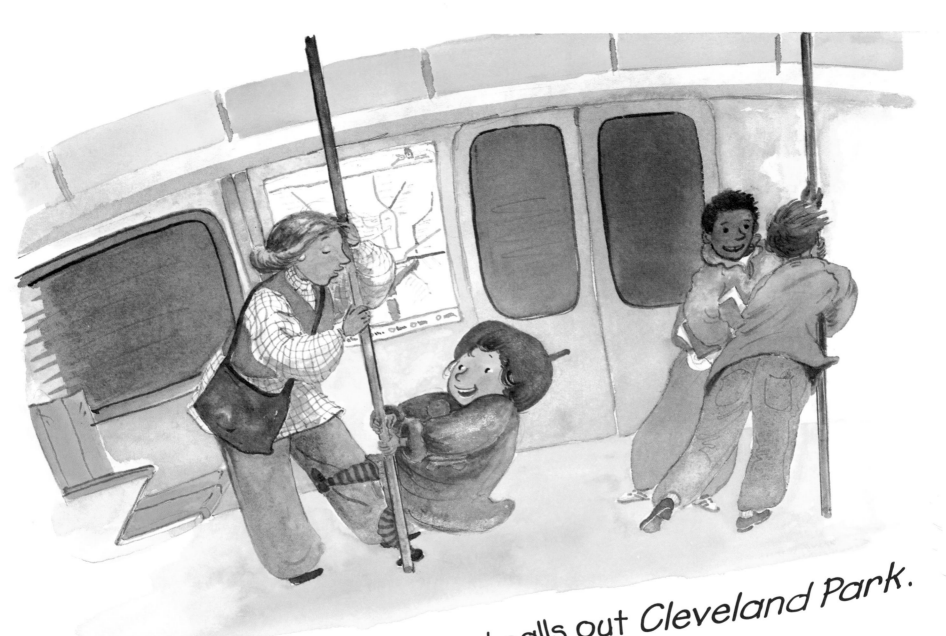

of dark until the driver halts and calls out *Cleveland Park.*

My stop.

The bright doors part. We walk beside the quiet train. I pay my fare. I step and sway

onto the stairs, which roll us up,
roll me and Mama up,
up, up until the sunshine streams
across the tangled streets,

the racing kids, the waiting geese;

and Nana waves at me.

Before I leave, I hear the sound
of something underground.

Below the earth, below *my* feet,
the train is gaining speed
and rushing to the nearest stop
where folks step on and off.

Rrrruuuummm. Whoooosshh.

And then it starts again, far down,
down, down in the underground.
Below the earth, below *my* shoes,

Rrrruuuummm. Whoooosshh.

the lighted train continues.